little brave

By Rose Sprinkle

Illustrations by Kimberli Johnson

RESOURCE *Publications* • Eugene, Oregon

Little Brave had no fear.
He was the bravest of all.
No monster could scare him,
No, not one at all.

All of the kingdom
loudly cheered of his tales.
"Little Brave the invincible,
His courage can't fail."

Little Brave was convinced.
He could only agree,
"I can never be hurt,
I fight so valiantly."

"I am the bravest,"
Or so he thought,
Until he met Dragon,
A foe he'd never fought.

"I am not afraid
Of you or any other.
You don't scare me,
So why even bother?"

"We shall see, Little Brave,
If your courage is true.
No knight has defeated me
And neither shall you."

Little Brave was fast,
But Dragon was faster.
He flew like a bullet.
The sky knew him as master.

Little Brave was strong,
But Dragon was stronger,
His fangs and claws sharp.
His tail whipped with bother.

Little Brave fought
The best that he could,

But Dragon outfought him
No matter how good.

"How can this be?
I've never lost in a fight!
Am I not Little Brave,
Most courageous of knights?"

As doubt turned to fear
And began to take sway,
Little Brave's heart
Shrank smaller that day.

The monsters he once
Could easily fight
Now outdid him in strength,
In wit, and in might.

With each battle he lost,
His heart grew smaller,
Until the sad day
He could stand it no longer.

"I am no brave knight.
I'm not brave at all.
I can't win my battles.
My heart is too small."

Then one fateful eve,
Dragon took flight.
His fire and terror filled
The dark of the night.

"Who will contend
With the mightiest of beasts?
Show me your champion,
One worthy at least."

The kingdom all cried
Once more for Little Brave.
"Help! Fight the dragon!
Be quick to save!"

But ashamed, Little Brave
Hung his head low.
Defeated, he whispered,
"I will not go."

The queen saw Little Brave,
His heart small with fright.
"Take courage, little one,
And finish the fight."

"You think to be brave
Is the absence of fear,
But you are mistaken,
misguided, unclear."

"A knight without fear
Doesn't know a true fight.
With no fear there's no valor,
No strength, and no might."

"Now arm yourself surely
With sword and with shield.
Meet Dragon in battle
And conquer your fear!"

Little Brave felt
A glimmer, a glow.
His heart, ever so slightly,
Began to grow.

"Why can't I be brave,
Have the courage to fight?
Even with a small heart,
I can do what's right."

"I will answer your challenge,
Dragon, at your request.
I may not defeat you
But will do my best."

Little Brave swung and sparred
And gave all that he could,
No matter if his swing
Was bad or was good.

The queen, now smiling,
Was pleased with delight
To see Little Brave
Stand firm in the fight.

"Bravo, Little Brave,
You are braver than ever!
To push through your fear
Is the bravest endeavor."

"True courage is not
To live without fear.
It is to fight
Even when it is near!"

And so Little Brave,
He learned in time,
Courage isn't the victory,
It's the will to try.

ABOUT THE AUTHOR

Rose Sprinkle is a published author that enjoys creating timeless stories for children and loves spending time with her two beagles and husband in the Pacific northwest. Check out www.thelittlevirtues.com to learn more about the books and follow on social media.

ABOUT THE ILLUSTRATOR

Kimberli Johnson specializes in watercolor and lives in Utah. She loves working with traditional materials and drawing woodland creatures. She gets inspiration from riding her horse and spending time in nature. You can check out her work on instagram at kimberlistudio.

Resource Publications, An Imprint of Wipf and Stock Publishers 199 W. 8th Ave., Suite 3 Eugene, OR 97401
www.wipfandstock.com

Cataloguing-in-Publication data:

Names: Sprinkle, Rose, author | Johnson, Kimberli, Illustrator
Title: Little Brave / Rose Sprinkle.
Description: Eugene, OR: Resource Publications, 2021
Identifiers: ISBN 978-1-5326-8915-4 (hardcover) | ISBN 978-1-5326-8916-1 (paperback) | ISBN 978-1-5326-8917-8 (ebook)
Subjects: LCSH: Children's Stories | Adventure and adventurers—Fiction | Coming of age—Fiction

CPSIA information can be obtained
at www.ICGtesting.com
Printed in the USA
JSHW040004280623
43832JS00006B/275